Rainbow Fish & Friends

A FISHY STORY

W9-BLN-383

TEXT BY GAIL DONOVAN

ILLUSTRATIONS BY DAVID AUSTIN CLAR STUDIO

Night Sky Books
New York • London

Rainbow Fish and his friends floated into the school cave.

"Attention, little fish!" said Miss Cuttle. "This morning a new friend will join us. Her name is Angel, and her family has just moved here from the Western Waters."

Puffer waved his fin wildly. "I've been *all* over the Western Waters!"

"Really?" said Miss Cuttle. "I'd love to hear about it. Will you share your story with us?"

"You've never seen anything like it," said Puffer.

"That does sound interesting," said Miss Cuttle, "but could you be a bit more specific?"

"The water is this weird . . . purple-blue!" he said. "And the plants are so huge—they grow from the ocean floor . . . all the way to the surface! And the rocks are in crazy . . . gigantic stacks! They think maybe some giant lobsters piled them up a long time ago."

"*Really?*" said Miss Cuttle. "Well, that's all we have time for now. I see our new friend is here."

Miss Cuttle asked Angel to tell the class about herself and the Western Waters.

"Well, the water is a dreamy green and is absolutely crystal clear, so you can see for miles and miles."

"I thought the water was purple-blue," said Rainbow Fish.

Angel shook her head no. The whole class turned to Puffer.

"I meant at sunset!" he cried. "The water goes all purple!"

Miss Cuttle put her tentacle around Puffer. "I love a good story," she said. "And I can see you do, too. Thank you for the tall tale, Puffer."

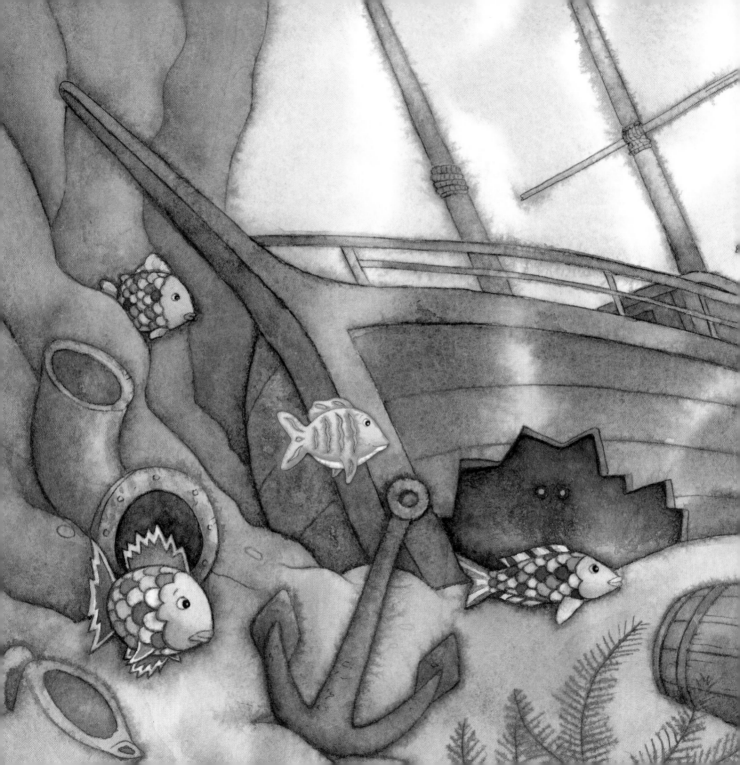

After lunch all of the fish went to play near the Sunken Ship.

"Come on," Rainbow Fish invited Angel. "We'll show you around."

"Hey, Puffer," said Tug, "tell Angel how the ship sunk!"

Everyone loved the story Puffer had told them of how the ship had come to rest outside the school cave. They all circled round him chanting, "Tell! Tell!"

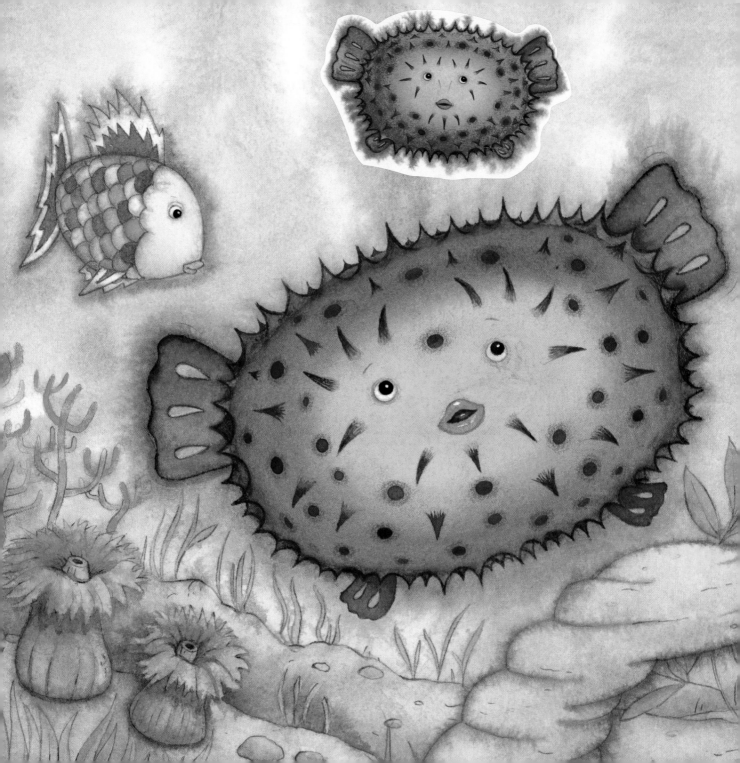

"It was a dark and stormy night," began Puffer, "and the captain of the ship knew they were carrying too heavy a load. If they were going to ride out the storm they would have to lighten the load. So he gave the command . . ."

"Throw the cargo overboard!" Angel chimed in. "Sorry, Puffer, I love that part. Go on, tell the rest."

"How did you know that?" asked Rainbow Fish.

"It's a famous story," said Angel, "about a sunken ship in the Butterfly Reef. We lived there when I was little."

"But, Puffer," said Tug, "you said that it happened here!"

"Maybe it's the same ship," suggested Pearl.

"Yeah, right!" said Spike.

"Maybe it drifted here," added Rusty, worried that his friends might start fighting.

"The prevailing currents go the other way," said Dyna. "A ship in the Butterfly Reef could never drift here, not in a million years."

"Puffer, what's the story?" asked Rainbow Fish. "The *real* story?"

While everyone waited for an explanation, Miss Cuttle rang the bell. Puffer was first into the cave.

"Let's look at the world of the Oyster Beds," said Miss Cuttle that afternoon. "Has anyone ever been to this fascinating place?"

Angel said, "I have."

"Me, too!" added Puffer. "We go there *all* the time!"

"Splendid," said Miss Cuttle, "I want to learn all about it. Angel, will you go first, please?"

"They're quite beautiful," said Angel. "There are oysters as far as the eye can see. And if even the teeniest, tiniest little grain of sand gets inside an oyster, it makes a pearl. The only problem is, it's terribly difficult to find a pearl. I looked and looked and never found a single one."

"I found a pearl!" Puffer said. "I found a whole bunch! *Hundreds!*"

Miss Cuttle smiled. "Look at my eight tentacles, Puffer. Now let's try to imagine twelve octopuses. We would have ninety-six tentacles altogether—*almost* a hundred. So how many pearls did you see?"

"Well, maybe it was more like ten . . . or nine . . . or eight."

"Maybe it was a big lie," said Rainbow Fish, and the others agreed. They were sure Puffer hadn't found any pearls. They were sure he'd never even been to the Oyster Beds.

"But I did go!" cried Puffer. "I really did!"

"Oh, right," said Rosie, "in your dreams."

"That's enough," said Miss Cuttle. "Maybe Puffer's imagination carried him away about the number of pearls, but if he says he went there, then he did. Class dismissed."

The next day, Miss Cuttle asked if anyone had anything for show-and-tell.

"I do!" said Puffer. Everyone groaned. Then Puffer held up something in front of the class.

"It's so shiny," said Rainbow Fish.

"It's huge," said Spike.

"It's true," said Pearl. "You really did find a pearl!"

Angel told Puffer it was the most beautiful pearl she'd ever seen.

"You mean it?" he asked. "You've seen so many. I bet you're exaggerating."

"I am not! You're the one who does that," she joked.

Puffer smiled. "You're right," he said. "I'm the biggest exaggerator there is!"

"Want to come over after school?" she asked. "I've got a fabulous book of sea stories we could look at."

"The one with the sunken ship story?" asked Puffer. "I've read it a *million* times! I'd love to come over."